Mama Seeton's Whistle

To the old gang on George Street
—JS

For Parnia, the mother of boys
—LP

• Little, Brown and Company • Hachette Book Group • 1290 Avenue of the Americas, New York, NY 10104 • Visit our website at lb-kids.com • Little, Brown and Company is a division of Hachette Book Group, Inc. • The Little, Brown name and logo are trademarks of Hachette Book Group, Inc. • The publisher is not responsible for websites (or their content) that are not owned by the publisher. • First Edition: April 2015 • Library of Congress Cataloging-in-Publication Data • Spinelli, Jerry. • Mama Seeton's whistle / by Jerry Spinelli ; illustrated by LeUyen Pham. — First edition. • pages cm • Summary: "Mama Seeton's simple and comforting whistle calls her family home, no matter how far away they may be"— Provided by publisher. • ISBN 978-0-316-12217-7 (hardcover) • [1. Whistling—Fiction. 2. Mother and child—Fiction. 3. Family life—Fiction.] I. Pham, LeUyen, illustrator. II. Title. • PZ7.S75663Mam 2015 • [E]—dc23 • 2013037876 • 10 9 8 7 6 5 4 3 2 1 • SC • Printed in China

MAMA SEETON'S WHISTLE

BY JERRY SPINELLI

ART BY LeUYEN PHAM

LB

LITTLE, BROWN AND COMPANY
NEW YORK BOSTON

The first whistle happened one day when Skippy Seeton was two years old. Mama Seeton came to the back door to call him in for dinner.

He wasn't there.

Mama Seeton was puzzled. From the kitchen window, she had been watching him play.

She stepped into the backyard and called again.

No one came.

Mama Seeton was worried.

And that's when it happened.

Without even thinking about it, Mama Seeton puckered her lips and whistled.

It was not a loud whistle.

Or a fancy whistle.

Just a simple, two-note whistle.

But to Skippy Seeton's ears, it was too wonderful to resist.

He popped up and piped, "I'm here, Mama!"
He had been hiding behind her the whole time.

Every day from then on, Skippy Seeton came to dinner when he heard his mother's whistle.

And that's how it was when little brother Sheldon came along.

And brother Stewart.

And finally a sister—Sophie.

Whenever the Seeton kids heard the whistle,
they came running from the backyard.

And from their friends' backyards.

And from the Beswicks' living room,
where they sat on the floor watching TV.

For these were the old days, when only
one family on a block had a TV.

Every day Mama Seeton baked a chocolate cake.

Every day by the end of dinner, it was gone.

As the Seeton kids got older, they played farther and farther from their own backyard.

They played in the alley.

They played to the end of the block.

They played all the way to Stony Creek.

Then across the creek
and into the park.

But they never went farther than Mama
Seeton's whistle. It always found them
and called them home for dinner—and
chocolate cake.

As the Seeton kids got older still, they traveled to all corners of town.

Skippy Seeton rode his bike to the North End, where he snacked in his favorite mulberry tree.

Sheldon Seeton rode his scooter downtown to visit Papa Seeton, who was a driver for Radio Taxi.

Stewart Seeton rolled his skateboard
to the park, where he made friends
with the monkeys
in the zoo.

Sophie Seeton ran—but she didn't go anywhere
in particular. She just loved to run.

And every day at dinnertime,
Mama Seeton whistled.

The whistle wasn't loud and it wasn't fancy. But it went in all directions. It flew through the talk of people and the noise of cars and buses.

Always it found the Seeton kids wherever they were. And home they came, biking and boarding, scooting and running.

Time passed.

The old days became the new days.

When the Seeton kids grew all the way up, they left town.

Because that's what grown-up kids do in the new days.

Skippy Seeton went north,
where he became a forest ranger.

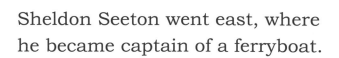

Sheldon Seeton went east, where
he became captain of a ferryboat.

Stewart Seeton went to Africa
to make the acquaintance
of mountain gorillas.

And Sophie Seeton—Sophie went
everywhere. Sophie ran marathon
races all over the world.

Of course, they were all too far away to come
home for dinner.

Every day Mama Seeton went to the back door.
But she did not whistle anymore.

She still baked a chocolate cake. But only
once a week.

Time went by, as time does.

"Our nest is empty!" cried Mama Seeton.

Papa Seeton tried to cheer her up. "Not really," he said. "We two old birds are still here."

Mama Seeton smiled, but it was a sad smile. She missed her children.

Of course, the Seeton kids missed their mother too. They wrote to her and sent pictures.

Every day at least one letter came through the mail slot in the front door.

But for Mama Seeton, it wasn't the same. She longed to touch a face—not an envelope.

Time and again she said, "I miss the old days."

One day Papa Seeton looked across the dining room table and saw that his wife had not touched her dinner. He had an idea.

He helped her up from her chair and led her to the back door.

"Okay," he said. "Whistle."

She gave him a look. "Are you goofy?"

"Not at all," he said. "If you just pretend it's the old days, maybe you'll feel a little better."

So Mama Seeton whistled. She had to try three times, for she was out of practice. The whistle was not loud. It was not fancy. Just a simple, two-note whistle.

But pretending did not make Mama Seeton feel better. No pretend children came running down the alley. All she felt was disappointment.

She went back inside and took a nap.

While Mama Seeton was napping, something happened that no one has ever been able to explain. Her out-of-practice whistle flew down the alley...

and through the neighborhood...

and through the town...

and across the country...

and around the world...

until it found every one of her children.

Skippy Seeton came down from his treetop ranger lookout.

Sheldon Seeton docked his ferryboat and left the first mate in charge.

Stewart Seeton waved "So long!" to his furry friends.

And Sophie Seeton veered away from her race and headed for the nearest airport.

Soon all four Seeton kids were cutting up chocolate cake and laughing with Mama Seeton. And Mama Seeton's days were both new and old, and she was happy once again.

Time went by, as time does.

And now the Seeton children have
children of their own. And when
they call them in for dinner,
they do it with a whistle.

It is not loud.

It is not fancy.

Just two simple notes
that fly through the
talk of people and
the noise of cars
and buses...

until they find...

every one...

AUTHOR'S NOTE

Yes, there was a real Mama Seeton. Her first name was Thelma, and she made the world's best chocolate cake. She was my neighbor as I was growing up in Norristown, Pennsylvania. She and her husband, Len, who drove a taxi, had a handful of kids. In those days, kids with free time scattered all over the West End, thus giving Mama Seeton a problem: how to get them all home for dinner? Her answer was her whistle. When the Seeton kids heard it, they came running. And so, to our own dinner tables, did the rest of us.　　　—*Jerry Spinelli*

ILLUSTRATOR'S NOTE

Jerry Spinelli is a master storyteller. While it's an incredible gift to illustrate such a lovely story, it's also incredibly intimidating. I quickly discovered that to make the illustrations match the depth of the writing, I had to think about the backstory of this woman—this entire family, in fact.

So I built a time line for the characters, figuring out just how old each character was when certain events occurred, how old Mama and Papa Seeton were when each child was born, even how many dogs the family would have had over the course of the book.

How much fun was it for an illustrator to figure out all this stuff? A *lot* of fun. I could determine what kind of clothes they would have worn, what kind of hairstyles they had, what the feeling of the era was. It's time travel, and I love it. It made the story so much more real to me to paint Papa proudly showing off his 1965 Chevrolet, to have period-style mailboxes and bicycles, to paint groovy hairstyles and flowing muumuus. And as the story reached its climax, with Mama Seeton yearning sweetly for her children, I found myself emotional along with her, because being a mother means being enveloped in such a range and depth of emotion through your children. Mama Seeton is a very real personification of motherhood, and I did my best to portray her with love.　　　—*LeUyen Pham*

ABOUT THIS BOOK

This book was edited by Alvina Ling and designed by Saho Fujii. The production was supervised by Erika Schwartz, and the production editor was Barbara Bakowski. This book was printed on 140-gsm Gold Sun wood-free paper. The illustrations were rendered in ink and watercolor on Arches hot-press paper.